When Is MY Birthday?

By Ray Sipherd
Illustrated by Tom Cooke

Featuring JIM HENSON'S SESAME STREET MUPPETS

A SESAME STREET/GOLDEN PRESS BOOK
Published by Western Publishing Company, Inc., in conjunction with Children's Television Workshop.

After Elmo's sister, Daisy, went off to school one day,
his mother said, "Guess what, Elmo. Tomorrow is
Daisy's birthday. She will be six years old!"

"Goody!" said Elmo. "I love birthdays!"

"Would you like to help me with the party?" asked his mommy.

"Oh, yes!" he said.

So Elmo helped Mommy wrap Daisy's birthday presents.

That afternoon a big mail delivery came to Elmo's house.

"Mommy, look at all the packages!" said Elmo.

"Yes," said Mommy. "These must be birthday presents for Daisy."

"Oh," he said.

"I will buy Daisy a birthday present, too," thought Elmo.

He took his piggy bank down from the shelf and emptied every last penny out of it.

"And I know just what I will get!"

When Elmo woke up the next morning, Daddy was busy blowing up balloons in the living room.

"'Hi, Elmo! Would you like to help me decorate for Daisy's party?" asked Daddy.

"Oh, yes!" said Elmo.

So Elmo and Daddy blew and blew.

"Whew!" Elmo gasped at last. "Blowing up balloons is hard work!"

Elmo and Mommy and Daddy set out party hats
and favors for the birthday guests.
   Then they hung up a big banner. HAPPY BIRTHDAY
DAISY it said.

Then it was time to bake the cake!

"Would you like to stir the batter, Elmo?" asked Mommy.

So Elmo mixed the batter and his mommy poured it into the cake pan. When the cake came out of the oven, they frosted it with pink icing.

"May I have a piece of cake now?" Elmo asked.

"No. I'm sorry, but we can't cut it until the party," Mommy said. "And this is Daisy's birthday cake, so she gets the first piece."

"Mommy," said Elmo as he stuck six candles on the cake, "when is *my* birthday?"

Just then the telephone rang. Elmo ran to answer it.
"Hello!" he said into the phone.

"Oh, hello, Elmo dear," answered Grandma. "Is Daisy
there? I want to wish her a happy birthday."

Elmo heard Daisy talking to Grandma. "Thank you,
Grandma!" she said. "I'm having a party and all my
friends are coming!"

At two o'clock the doorbell rang as the party guests began to arrive.

"Hi, Elmo," they said.

"Happy birthday, Daisy!" they said.

Friends and relatives crowded around Daisy and gave her birthday hugs and kisses.

They told her what a big girl she was getting to be.
They took pictures of the birthday girl.

They played duck, duck, monster and musical monster chairs and blindmonster's buff.

Then it was time for Daisy to
open her birthday presents.
    "Elmo," said his mommy.
"'Would you like to be the first to
give Daisy her present?"
    Elmo handed Daisy the big
bunch of beautiful yellow daisies
he had bought with all the
money in his piggy bank.
    "Happy birthday, Daisy," he said.

Daisy opened her other birthday presents—a paint set, a comb and brush, some storybooks, and toys, toys, toys.

The last present was a toy truck.

It was the most wonderful toy truck Elmo had ever seen.

"You lucky duck!" he said to Daisy.

Elmo carried the beautiful birthday cake out of the kitchen and put it on the table in front of Daisy. The six candles burned brightly on top.

"Make a wish," Mommy said to Daisy. "And if you blow out all the candles at once, your wish will come true."

So Daisy took a deep breath and blew out all the candles! Everybody cheered and clapped their hands.

"Now your wish will come true!" Elmo said to Daisy.

Elmo made a wish, too. He wished
for the toy truck.
Suddenly Elmo didn't want any
birthday cake after all.

When Daisy's guests began to play pin-the-nose-on-the-monster, Elmo just watched. Daisy came over and sat beside him.

"I really like the daisies, Elmo," she said.

Then she asked, "Would you like to play with my new truck?"

"Gee, thanks!" said Elmo.

Later, when all the party guests had gone home, Elmo and Daisy played with the truck together.

"When is *my* birthday?" asked Elmo.

"Your birthday is one week after mine," said Daisy. "That's only seven days away! And I know just what you want!"

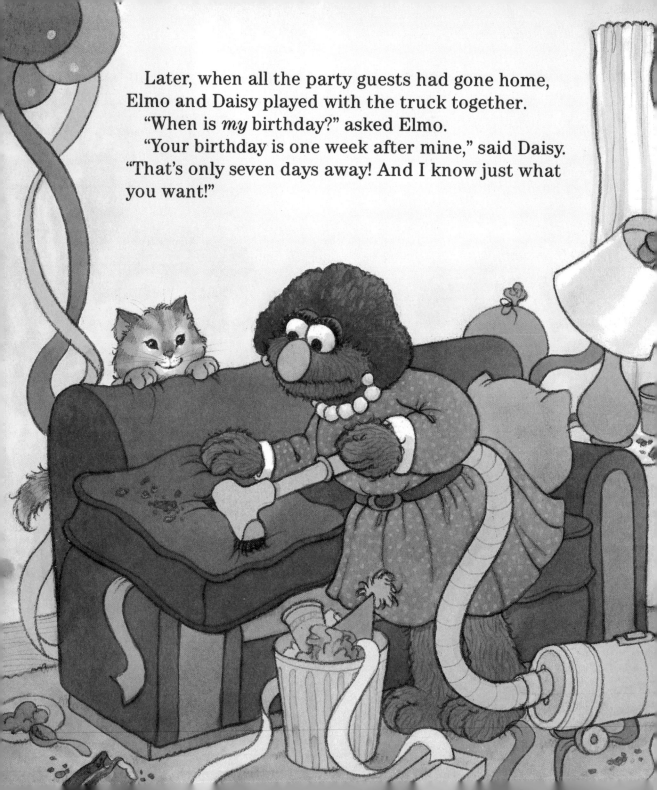